About the ONCE UPON AMERICA® Series

Who is affected by the events of history? Not only the famous and powerful. Individuals from every part of society contribute a *story*—and so weave together *history*. Some of the finest storytellers bring their talents to this series of historical fiction, based on careful research and designed specifically for readers ages 7–11. These are tales of young people growing up in a young, dynamic country. Each ONCE UPON AMERICA® volume shapes readers' understanding of the people who built America and of their own roles in our unfolding history. For history is a story that we continue to write, with a chapter for each of us beginning "Once upon America."

Earthquake!

A STORY OF OLD SAN FRANCISCO

BY KATHLEEN V. KUDLINSKI

ILLUSTRATED BY RONALD HIMLER

SCHOLASTIC INC.
New York Toronto London Auckland Sydney

*Many thanks to Professor Howell Smith, Chairman of the History Department,
Wake Forest University; Pat Haines, Director of SJ Ranch Riding Camp; and Julie
Morton, Camp Horsemanship Association Certified Trainer; who all read this text
for background authenticity; and a special thanks to Barbara Kenney.*

ISBN 0-590-67303-3

24 23 22 21 20 19 18 17 16 15   4 5 6 7 8 9/0

Printed in the U.S.A.   40

First Scholastic printing, November 1995

For my daughter,
Betsy, who has a way with horses
and with people

Contents

Howling in the Night

"Oh, be quiet, Buster," Phillip grumbled into his pillow. "Stupid dog." He pulled the covers over his head. But something about the old retriever's barking would not let him go back to sleep.

Phillip listened. This wasn't Buster's deep, growling "rrraouf"—the one that meant *Stranger*. It wasn't the higher, quick bark that called *Hi, friend!* It wasn't the toneless, patient "woof" that meant *I have to go out*. This was different.

Pastor Olson's dog sounded scared.

And the blind cocker spaniel down at Taylor's Bakery was whining, too.

Phillip sat up and leaned into the dark and silent bedroom. Through the open window, he could hear dogs all over San Francisco. Some were barking, some were howling, and some were yapping, listening, then yapping again. From the chorus of howls to the south, it seemed that every dog in the pound was wide awake. By now, so was Phillip.

A horse whinnied sharply from the stable next door. "Linen?" Phillip said into the quiet bedroom. He thought he knew the voice of every horse in their stable, but this sounded strange. He heard the restless thud of hooves in deep hay. Phillip shoved his feet into slippers, threw on a pair of overalls, and ran out his bedroom door.

He didn't stop to turn on the gaslight in the hall. Moving through the dark house felt right, as if it were a normal morning, and chores were about to begin. What time was it?

Phillip's fingertips brushed down the long stair railing. "Thirteen, fourteen." He counted the stairs in a whisper, them jumped stair number fifteen, the one that squeaked. He didn't want to wake Chester. Whenever his four-year-old brother woke up early, he fussed until Papa let him help with the chores.

Moonlight slanted through the cut glass windows

on both sides of the front door. Phillip stopped at the grandfather clock and squinted up at its pale face. A little after four. Dawn would be in an hour, Phillip thought. He ripped the old calendar page off the pad. It was part of his chores to begin the next day, every day. *April 18, 1906*, he read silently.

He heard the sharp neighs and scuffle of a horse fight in the stable next door. Linen again? And *Shimmer*? But they were the stable's calmest team! Phillip turned and hurried through the house to the back door, his slippers silent on the deep carpet.

He grabbed his work boots off the back stoop and ran to the stable. As Phillip reached for the door handle something ran across his slipper. He jumped and peered at the road. One little dark body scurried through the moonlight, then another shot out from under the door. What were they? Another, even smaller, bumped into Phillip's ankle and fell back, stunned. Phillip gently picked it up. It was a baby mouse!

He cradled it in his hand and watched as half a dozen more mice fled through the crack under the door. What had them so frightened? Phillip wondered. A cat, he decided. There had to be a cat chasing them. He opened the door slowly, his foot ready to block the cat's escape.

There was no cat.

There was just moonlight, the whimpering of the blind cocker spaniel, the restless pawing of horses' hooves, and a strange stampede of mice.

Phillip set the baby down gently into the hay. "There, little fella." It turned in a confused circle, then ran outside. Phillip reached for the lantern on its hook inside the door. He lit it and turned the flame up high.

Ten stalls stretched before him. Horses looked over every door, blinking in the sudden light. Linen whickered at him from the nearest stall. Her eyes were wide. Phillip made himself be calm as he put the lantern back on its hook. "Easy girl," he said, his voice deep and soft. "Easy." He rubbed first her nose, then her warm cheek. She threw back her head, and then grew quiet. Phillip let himself into the stall and stood stroking her broad white neck.

"Settle down now. Easy does it." Phillip talked to her, to them all. Outside, the dogs barked on and on. "Whoa there, Pie. Hush, Ginger," Phillip called softly to the team of bays, pawing in their corner stalls. They settled down, as Phillip knew they would. That's how it always was with animals, Phillip thought. He leaned against Linen.

That's how it was when *he* was with animals, he corrected himself. Five minutes with Chester and the whole stable was in an uproar. Even Papa left them tense sometimes. But his father *was* good with them,

Phillip thought quickly. He had built a good business.

Phillip glanced through the door of the stall at the new sign drying in the corner. MACMILLAN AND SON LIVERY STABLE it said in gold script. BICYCLE REPAIR was printed below in black. Papa had said they would hang it over the stable door after he gave it one last coat of varnish.

A scraping sound came from the next stall, where Misty pawed the floor. A horse farther down the row rattled its water bucket. Calm, Phillip told himself. Stay calm. Distant dogs howled on into the morning.

"What's going on here?" Papa's voice boomed from the stable door.

Phillip wanted to run to him, to bury his face in Papa's waistcoat, to smell the Papa smells: cigar smoke, after-shave, and horses. Four-year-old Chester could do that, Phillip reminded himself. At twelve, he was too old. "I couldn't sleep, Papa." He carefully closed the door of Linen's stall behind him.

Didn't you hear them? he wanted to ask. Didn't you hear the dogs? Or the horses? Did you see a cat when you came in? But Papa was already shoveling out the first stall, beginning the morning chores. As if nothing at all was wrong, Phillip thought. He grabbed a shovel, hoping his father was right.

He listened to the comfortable *scrape* and *plop*, *scrape* and *plop*, as he and Papa mucked out the stalls together. When he finished his row, Phillip brought

Duchess's bucket to the spigot above the big watering trough. He filled it and left the water running. He opened her stall door and reached in to hang the bucket, and the world tilted.

Phillip grabbed for the wall, but the floor was where the wall should have been. Water from the bucket splashed down over his head, and Duchess began to fall over toward him. Phillip tried to crawl away, but the horse landed on his legs. A scream filled Phillip's ears, his world. Was it his own scream or the horse's? Phillip couldn't tell.

Earthquake!

Phillip fought to get his legs free. The weight and heat of the big mare were too much to bear. He punched at her side. "Get off!" he yelled.

Duchess was trying. She gathered one leg beneath her to heave herself to her feet, when the earth tilted again. She flopped against the far wall of the stall, a giant rag doll of a horse, and landed with a sickening *crunch*. Before she hit the ground, Phillip scrambled out of her way and rolled out through the stall door.

Timbers were screeching and splintering and the floorboards groaned. The air was filled with a *roar* Phillip could feel in his teeth. The church bell from the corner rang wildly. Who was ringing it? He reached for the floor to push himself to his feet and clawed at empty air instead. Where was the ground? His body hit the side of the watering trough, then thumped against the floor.

Phillip lay for a moment, fighting for breath. Beneath his knees, he could feel the wooden floor of the stable trembling. His body was shaking along with the earth. It bounced his head against the floor, then the water trough, then the floor again. Phillip looked around in the wildly flickering lantern light for something to hold on to, but everything was moving. "Papa!" he called into the roaring confusion.

The shrill whinnies of terrified horses filled the stable. Their big bodies thumped heavily against the walls of their stalls as the earth shifted again and again beneath their feet. The horses fought for balance, pounding their hooves against the floor. "Papa?" Phillip yelled as loud as he could.

"It's an earthquake, son!" Papa yelled back from across the stable. "Stay down. She can't last forever."

Water sloshed over the edge of the trough and soaked Phillip. And then it was quiet.

Phillip held his breath. Everything was still.

The quiet lasted only a heartbeat before Duchess screamed in pain. Linen whinnied and snorted. The others danced and whickered in their stalls.

"See to the horses!" His father's voice carried over the sounds of the frantic animals. "I'm going to your mother!"

And he was gone. Phillip got to his feet, groaning from a thousand bruises.

Linen whinnied and nuzzled him roughly when he reached her. He threw his arms around her neck and hid his face against her warm skin. Squeezing his eyes shut, he pressed his cheek into the strong muscles of her neck. Linen shifted and whickered.

"Easy girl," he heard himself say. His voice sounded calm and distant. "Easy now. Everything's going to be all right." Everything was not all right, and he knew it, but his voice kept going on and on.

Pie and Ginger stood trembling as Phillip rubbed his hands down their legs. Pie lashed out with a rear hoof. "I won't touch it again," Phillip promised, "but you're already swelling there." He would have to get some wrappings off the shelf.

Papa would want a complete report on the horses, Phillip knew—who was hurt, where, and how badly. He had to keep moving to cover all the stalls, but he didn't want to go too fast. He didn't want to miss anything.

Misty and Joe had bloody, tender spots on their legs,

too. Nothing serious. "I'll wipe you down with those soft old grain bags," he murmured. "And cool water. That will feel fine."

Phillip entered the next-to-last stall. Stormy was standing with his weight on three legs. A bloody metal bucket lay trampled by his hooves. "Oh, fella, what have we got here?" Phillip looked at a jagged cut on Stormy's fetlock. He grabbed a handful of feed bags and pressed one tightly over the cut.

Blood pulsed through the cloth and dripped between his fingers. Phillip added another layer of bags over the cut and then another. Stormy tried to jerk free, but Phillip hung on. He squeezed the leg so tightly that he lost the feeling in his fingers. Finally the bleeding slowed. Then it stopped. Phillip knew better than to peek at the cut. He tied the mess of bloody cloths against Stormy's leg and moved on to Duchess's stall. He looked at her over the door.

The fine old mare was lying on her side. She turned her head toward him, blinking groggily. "Take it easy, old girl," Phillip said. He remembered the sickening crunch he had heard, inches from his head. The mare lay with two of her long slender legs bent at odd angles. One was folded backward beneath her. The other lay limply crooked. The bloody end of a broken bone glinted in the dawn light from the stable door. Phillip knew there was nothing he could do for her. How am I going to tell Papa? he wondered.

Phillip turned and reached to blow the lantern out—when the stable floor jerked under his feet. Another quake? Not again! he thought wildly. He grabbed for the nearest stall door, but it was already over. The horses danced in their stalls, snorting nervously. An aftershock, he told himself. Just an aftershock. He'd heard about them.

"Rest easy, fellas. The worst is over," he said. "Nothing to worry—" Another sharp shock nearly knocked him off his feet. It did knock the lantern off its peg.

Phillip lunged across the stable, trying to catch the lantern before it fell. He was too late. It bounced once against the wooden floor and came to rest by a bale of hay. Fuel splashed out where the lantern hit. By the time Phillip got to it, a puddle of the kerosene fuel had leaked onto the floor. With a *whoosh*, the puddle burst into flame, and the flame scampered outward toward the dry hay. Toward Phillip. Toward the horses.

Fire!

Phillip had dipped a bucket into the big water trough before he even knew what he was doing. They'd practiced this. Barn fire. The greatest horror of any stablemaster. Dry hay, dry straw, feed sacks, and old wood, plus well-oiled leather—and nothing to stop it all from burning to ashes, along with the horses trapped inside.

Phillip threw the bucketful of water toward the fire. Over and over he scooped, twisted, threw, and scooped again, until the blaze was all out.

He scattered the straw with the toe of his boot and sprinkled water on every inch of the floor. Steam and smoke and the sounds of frantic horses filled the stable.

But the fire was out. "That's all for today, fellas." Phillip laughed and wondered why he was laughing. He shook his head. "Quiet down, now. Easy." He paused beside every stall to rub the horses' faces, to calm them. "The worst that can happen has happened," he told them. "At least the worst I can think of."

He looked over the door at Duchess and bit his lip as she neighed a weak greeting from the floor. He wanted to run to the house, to see Mama. Why wasn't Papa back? Had something happened to Chester?

He hurried to the stable doorway, then froze. Everywhere he looked, something was broken. The neighbor's chimney had fallen across the sidewalk. Birdbaths and porch chairs were lying where they'd been thrown by the earthquake. Shutters dangled in the wind, and broken windows glinted in the early morning sun. He could hear the sounds of babies crying, of dogs barking, and—strangely—of birds singing.

The porch of the minister's house across the street looked crooked somehow. As Phillip watched, it toppled forward with a great splintering crash. Dust and dirt flew from beneath it. Buster started barking desperately. Pastor Olson opened his door and stopped just before he fell into the ruins. He stood in the empty doorway in silence, staring at the space where his porch had been.

This looks like a dream, Phillip thought. A bad one. Pastor Olson was wearing his pajamas and nightcap. His arms hung limp at his sides. Phillip had never seen him without a suit and starched collar. Now there he was in blue-and-white striped nightclothes, in full view of everyone on the street. A tassel hung from his nightcap. It swung in time with the slow shaking of his head.

Phillip wanted to wave—to say something—but what was there to say?

Bobby Hunt appeared in the doorway and threw his arms around the pastor. Bobby was crying. Crying! The Bobby Hunt who used words like *gad!* and *Jehoshaphat!* right in school. The Bobby Hunt who tied broken glass to his kite strings to cut off everybody else's kites in the sky. The Bobby Hunt who kicked the blind cocker spaniel when he thought nobody was looking.

Phillip looked down so he wouldn't have to watch Bobby Hunt cry. The trolley tracks in the road in front of him lay twisted and ripped from the pavement. How would the trolley cars get through? How could horses drive their buggies over the jagged metal? What would happen now?

What had happened at his own house? Phillip held his breath and stepped out to look next door. Home was standing tall and straight. The chimneys were both

still there. The front porch wasn't sagging, either, Phillip thought—not one bit. At least his own house was safe. He breathed deeply.

Where was Papa? Phillip wanted him to come right to the door like Pastor Olson did. He had to tell him about the fire. About the horses. About Duchess. He fought against the wish to run to his house. There was one more barn chore he had to do.

The water trough had to be filled again. "Never leave a stable dry," he quoted Papa to the horses as he walked past their stalls. After the lantern fire, he knew he would never forget that rule again.

He leaned over the empty trough and turned on the tap. No water came out. He turned the knob all the way and all the way back. Nothing. No gush. No trickle. Not even a gurgle way back in the pipes. There was no water.

In the silence, Phillip heard fire bells clanging all over San Francisco.

All That
Matters

"Mama, Mama," Phillip kept saying. "You're all right!" He buried his face in the lace on her collar. He breathed in her lavender perfume, but the smoke and stink of the stable still filled his mind. And the blood.

"The horses, Mama," he said. "The horses are hurt. And Duchess . . ."

"*Shhhh.* All of us are safe, dear," Mama said. Her cheek was pressed hard on the top of Phillip's head. "And that's all that matters."

Phillip had been stepping carefully across the lawn toward the house. What if there is another aftershock? he had kept thinking. Or another earthquake? He didn't want to hit his head on anything sharp when he fell. The fence posts, the stakes that held up Mama's flowers, even the cement birdbath had looked dangerous. Phillip's steps had slowed even more.

Then Mama had come out onto the front porch. Somehow, suddenly, Phillip was across the lawn, up the porch stairs, and in her arms before he'd thought about the danger. Now here she was, smelling like herself, and telling him that everything was all right. The earthquake was over.

"Broke! It's all broke!" Chester wailed from inside the house.

Phillip pulled away to see what was wrong with his little brother. "Wait," Mama said. She held Phillip's shoulders and looked into his eyes. "Remember, darling. We are all safe." There were tears in her eyes. "Nothing—*nothing*—else matters." Phillip pulled free and rushed past her through the doorway.

And stopped.

Broken glass covered the carpet from one side of the front hall to the other. Where had it come from? Phillip looked up. The chandelier! Most of the glass crystals had been tossed off during the earthquake. He shook his head slowly. It had taken hours to wash all those crystals. He and Mama had polished each one. How it had sparkled when the gaslights were lit! Mama had danced right in the middle of the hall. "Just for the beauty of it," she had said.

Broken crystals crunched under his feet as he walked over to look down at the grandfather clock. It was lying on its side on the carpet. Phillip picked up the minute hand and held it between his fingers. The clock's long brass pendulum lay bent at a strange angle. Worst of all, the clock was silent. For as long as Phillip could remember, it had ticked through his days. It had chimed every hour and quarter hour of his life. And now it was silent.

How would he know what time it was if he awoke in the night? Phillip wondered. Or whether it was time for chores? A tinkling sound came from over his head. He looked up. The few crystals left in the chandelier were swaying. Philip had barely felt that aftershock.

Chester ran into the front hall. "He won't let me go upstairs," he complained. "It's not fair!"

"Who won't?" Phillip asked, confused.

"Papa."

Phillip crunched over to the stairs and headed up. "Papa?" he called. "The horses need you!"

"That you, Phillip?" Papa called from a bedroom. "Stay off the stairs." It was too late. Phillip was halfway up, clinging to the railing. The whole staircase creaked under his weight as it sagged further and further away from the wall. The wallpaper ripped slowly beside him. A crack in the plaster beneath the wallpaper widened as he watched, and plaster dust trickled out.

This can't be happening, Phillip thought. Walls don't break. He moved to the outside of the stairs, as far as he could get from the wall. There was a *screech* of nails pulling out of dry wood.

"Get off!" Papa thundered from above him. Phillip ran down, jumping the last five stairs. "Catch!" he heard. He turned to see armfuls of clothes flying down through the air at him.

Phillip caught what he could. Papa's overalls. Chester's nightshirt. Mama's best dress. "I'll take them," Mama said, at his elbow. "Chester, you help me pack."

Pack? Phillip had no time to think about what she meant. Papa was throwing things down to him as fast as he could catch them. Papa's shaving brush. Mama's little jewelry box. Chester's toy automobile.

"Give me!" Chester said, pulling his treasure out of Phillip's hands.

"Stop, Papa," Phillip called. "Misty is hurt! And Duchess . . ." His voice broke. "Please, Papa!"

"Never mind the horses," Papa roared. "We've got to clear out."

Never mind the horses? Papa couldn't have said that! A cigar box opened as it flew toward him, dropping cigars and spreading the rich scent of tobacco down the stairs. The money bag from the stable was

next. It was so heavy Phillip almost dropped it. They had that many gold coins? Mama's favorite vase was next. It slipped from his hand and broke with the crystals on the carpet. "Oh, Mama!" he cried.

She looked up from the bag where she was stuffing clothes. "We're all safe," she said firmly. "That's all that matters." But there were tears running down her cheeks.

"Look up, Phillip," Papa called, and threw another armful down to him. And another. And then there wasn't any more. Just Papa standing at the top of the sagging staircase. How was he going to get down?

"What are you looking at?" Papa yelled. He sounded angry. "Get that mess out onto the lawn." Phillip stood, helpless, while a handful of plaster fell out of the wall and tumbled down the stairs. "Move!" shouted Papa.

Phillip moved. He grabbed what he could and hurried out the door, helping Mama and Chester pull the clothes bag across the porch floor. Behind him he heard a huge splintering crash, the sound of broken glass, and an oath.

Mama stood suddenly, her hand over her mouth. Her eyes were wide. Phillip froze. Chester ran back into the house. "Oh, no, Papa!" they heard him yell. "Your pants are split!"

Papa walked out onto the porch, holding his hands wide. A scratch on his cheek was just beginning to bleed and he was covered with plaster dust. "As you can see," he said, "my pants are, indeed, split. But," he added, "nothing else is." Phillip started to grin. Mama chuckled. And then the laughter began.

They laughed while they carried the last unbroken treasures out. They laughed while the house creaked and groaned, and plaster dust rained on them from the ceilings. They laughed until real tears fell. And then Papa would walk past, and it all seemed funny again.

Finally Papa pulled on his overalls. "Enough," he said to them, smoothing his moustache. "We need some breakfast. It's going to be a long day."

Mama turned to go back through the house, but Papa said, "We'd better go around." They headed to the back door of the kitchen. The brothers sat side by side on the front steps.

"Isn't this fun?" Chester said. He pushed his automobile back and forth on the stair. Phillip just stared at the ground. The stairs were lying inside, in a pile of twisted boards and torn carpet. There was no way he could get to his own room. His new kite was up there. So was his pocketknife. Phillip swallowed hard. His Bible was up there, too. And his clothes.

"*Brrrm, brrrm, brrrm,*" Chester said, pushing his toy automobile down the front path.

Papa's Gifts

Phillip bit into his favorite sandwich. It was bologna and cheese on Mama's own fresh bread. He was chewing a big mouthful of it, but he couldn't taste anything at all.

"We'll eat first," Papa had said when he had tried to tell him about the horses. "We can talk later." So Phillip sat, chewing on a bologna and cheese sandwich, while Pie's leg swelled. While Stormy tried to shake the bandage off her cut. While Duchess lay dying in her stall.

This has to be a dream, he thought. Please.

"Look, Phillip." Chester stood to get a better view. "Look at that ugly baby!"

"Chester!" Phillip hissed. But then he looked. A man was wheeling a baby carriage up the street. It was filled with clothes and shoes. A sewing machine sat on top. A woman in a ball gown walked along beside.

Behind them walked a family pulling a wagon. As far as Phillip could see down Van Ness Street, people were walking up, away from the center of town. Some were dressed in their finest clothes. Some were still in pajamas. All of them carried or dragged or pushed belongings.

Phillip looked at their faces. No one looked back at him. No one smiled. They didn't talk, even to one another. Phillip began to feel sick to his stomach. They all looked gray and confused and tired. And they just kept walking past, moving in a slow, sad stampede out of San Francisco.

"Here comes an automobile!" Chester squealed and ran to the fence. How could Chester be so happy about a stinking automobile, Phillip wondered, after all that has happened? But Chester seemed like the only real live person out there on Van Ness.

At least our family looks normal, Phillip thought. They were all eating silently now, but Mama and Papa had been laughing and talking after the earthquake. They all had. The earthquake hadn't hurt them at all.

Phillip turned to watch a fine pair of dapple grays picking their way over the twisted trolley tracks. They shied at the sound of the automobile engine heading up the street.

As it chugged past, the smell of its smoke hung in the air. Phillip tried not to breathe until the exhaust was all gone. He hated that smell.

But the smoke didn't go away. It just got thicker. Fire bells clanged nearby. No one ran to see. No one ran to help. No one even looked up.

"So, Phillip," Papa said, "how are the horses?"

He sounded as if it were just a normal day, Phillip thought. Don't you know what's happened, he wanted to yell. Our *business* is the stable! MacMillan and Son. And the stable *is* the horses. What was wrong with his father?

He made himself calm and said, "Stormy is cut bad, Papa, but she will be fine. Linen and the bays are scraped up some on the legs. Nothing serious." He paused. "But Duchess is down."

"How bad?"

"Two broken legs." Phillip could only whisper.

"Well, why didn't you say so?" Papa stood suddenly. Phillip got up to follow him to the stable, but Papa turned quickly and headed back into the house.

"Herbert!" Mama cried.

"I forgot something," Papa called from inside. He

brushed past Phillip on his way out again and strode toward the stable. Phillip tried to keep up, but his legs were too short. He had just reached the front gate when he heard the sound of a gunshot from inside the stable.

No! Phillip's knees gave way, and he grabbed for the gatepost to keep from falling. He made himself walk on into the stable. The stink of gunpowder hung in the air. Papa was bringing a harness out of the tack room. Things are moving too fast, Phillip thought.

"Get the bays ready, son," Papa said. "We'll hitch them to the buggy."

"But their legs . . ."

"Are they lamed?" Papa asked quickly.

"I don't know. I don't think so."

"They'll do then," Papa said. "They're the best team. I'll be taking your mother and Chester to Aunt Eleanor's until things are settled up here."

Phillip felt dizzy. "What about me?"

"You stay and mind the stable. Leave the CLOSED sign up and don't open for anybody or anything. I'll be back in a couple of days at the most."

"But Papa . . ."

"The house could drop on us any minute. Somebody has to stay with the horses. You."

Phillip led the bays out of their stalls and helped harness them to the buggy in silence. He drove them around to the front gate and waited until Mama climbed on and took the reins. Then he helped Papa lift all the bags and boxes into the back. He didn't say anything. There was nothing to say.

"Bye-bye!" Chester waved with a big grin. Mama gave Phillip a kiss and a long, fierce hug.

"Don't go into the house," Papa told him. "It's not safe now." He pulled himself up onto the buggy seat. "Oh, and here," he said, handing Phillip a grain bag. "You may need this."

Phillip reached up for the bag. Whatever was in it clanked like loose stirrups and bits. Why would he need those? he wondered. Phillip waved as the buggy pulled out into the street and joined the stream of people fleeing the city.

Back up on the porch, he emptied the grain bag into his lap. Philip sat looking at Papa's gifts and shaking his head. In a pile in his lap were five gold coins—and Papa's gun.

A heavy crash came from down the street. Phillip knew the sound of a staircase falling to the floor. The noise of a porch crashing to the ground. But this sound was much, much louder. Could a whole building just fall down?

Could his own house fall?

Phillip looked into his front hall. Sunlight sparkled on broken glass at each side of the door. He made himself go in and look at the fallen clock again. The crack in the wall where the stairs had been was much

wider now, and a creaking sound echoed in the empty hall.

He turned to go out and caught sight of himself in the hall mirror. There was a great crack through the glass. It made his face look broken in two. Both of the Phillips in the mirror had soot and ash on their faces, a smear of dried blood, and sweat. And under all of that, both Phillips looked gray and confused and tired, just like the people on the street outside.

Alone

Phillip sat alone on the front steps. The sound of fire bells floated up from all over town. What could the firemen be doing without water? Phillip wondered. There had to be water somewhere in the city. At least he hoped so. He had checked the faucets and there was none at all in the house.

The deep booming sounds he heard from the porch confused him at first. Then, in a moment of quiet, he heard gas hissing out of the broken chandelier in the hall behind him. Phillip grabbed his father's bundle and ran down the porch steps. If there was a spark in there, he thought, the explosion would blow him right off the porch. And set the whole house on fire.

It was then that Phillip realized what all those distant booming sounds were. He hurried on toward the stable. There was no water there, but there were no gas lines there, either.

He let the hot wind blow the stable door shut behind him. He pushed the bolt into place. Phillip took a deep breath. The wind had blown away most of the stink of the fire. In its place was the good smell of horses and clean hay. The stable was dim and cool after the heat of the sun. And it was quiet. Unless he listened hard, Phillip couldn't hear the fire alarms, the crashes, and the explosions. He tried not to listen at all.

He grabbed the broom and attacked the mess on the stable floor. He swept wildly, filling the air with hay dust and ashes. Phillip sneezed and swept even harder, getting rid of all of it. Making the stable right again. Making everything right again.

Linen snorted loudly next to his elbow and Phillip jumped. "Hey, girl," he said, then coughed on a mouthful of dust. He leaned the broom against her stall door. Linen reached her head out to nuzzle his ear. "Sorry, Linen." He rubbed her nose. "I guess I'm just making things worse."

He went down the row of stalls and gave each horse

an extra measure of grain. Each horse got an extra measure of love, too. Phillip rubbed Linen's neck where she liked it best. He scratched behind Black's ears until she shook her head with pleasure. He rubbed Shimmer's soft muzzle and stroked Beauty's broad black cheeks. At every stall, he talked low and gentle nonsense to settle the horses.

He tried not to think about Duchess.

He scooped the little water left in the trough and rubbed down each horse's legs. Stormy's cut started bleeding again when Phillip took the bandages off— but only a little. He tied clean cloths firmly in place. "Papa will take care of that," he promised him, "when he gets home." Home. Did he have one? Phillip pushed those thoughts out of his mind and hurried to the next stall. And the next.

Then he took the horses out, one by one. He pulled their halters off the pegs by each stall and slid them over the horses' heads. When they were tied to the wall, he scrubbed at their coats with a curry comb. The horse hair flew as he worked over the animals, soothing and rubbing their muscles as well as their coats. Next, he brushed them till they shone and led them back to their stalls.

He tried not to look at Duchess's stall.

What next? he thought. What can I do next? All the saddles, the harnesses, the reins, and the leathers in the tack room could be polished. The sign needs another coat of varnish. The windows need washing and the wagons could be cleaned up. Phillip smiled. There was a whole day's work here in the cool quiet.

His stomach grumbled. "Hush," he told it, and reached for the broom again to sweep the floor. This time he swept carefully, pushing a growing mound of horse hair and straw toward the back door of the stable. He threw the door open and knocked the dusty pile out with one final, wild sweep of the broom.

"Hey!" a voice yelled. A handful of horsehair flew back at Phillip. "What do you think you're doing?"

Phillip blinked at the dust and the sudden sunlight in his eyes. Bobby Hunt? Here? "I'm working," he snapped. "What are you doing on my back stoop?"

"Pastor told me to come over here."

"What?" That didn't make any sense. Pastor Olson has to know how much I hate Bobby, Phillip thought. He knows everything about me—about everybody in his church.

"The Craigs' whole house gave way in the quake," Bobby explained. "Mrs. Craig died right away, and the baby is hurt bad. Pastor went to help."

"Where's Mrs. Olson?" Phillip asked.

"She went on down to the church. There's a lot of folks there who can't stay in their houses."

Phillip thought about the big crack growing in the wall of his home. And the deadly hiss of gas. "But why did they send you *here?*" he asked.

"Well . . ." Bobby began. "They didn't. I'm supposed to stay in the house. And answer the telephone in case somebody else needs the pastor."

"You have a telephone?"

"Yes. But it doesn't work. And there isn't any water, either. And the fire alarms keep ringing." Bobby's voice choked. He looked off into the sky. "I just didn't want to be alone," he said. His voice was very little.

"Why?" This didn't sound like Bobby Hunt at all. "You scared of fire bells?"

"My mama and papa died in a fire," Bobby said. Now his voice was angry. "Didn't you know? That's why I had to come stay with the Olsons."

Phillip swallowed, hard. Nobody had known that. The kids at school said Bobby was so bad his folks didn't want him anymore. That his own parents had sent him away to live with a minister. The way Bobby acted, it had made sense.

Now Phillip remembered how scared Bobby had looked, crying in the doorway against the pastor's pajama sleeve.

"You want to clean the leathers with me?" he asked.

Bobby looked at him for a moment. "Thanks" was all he said.

They sat together on hay bales in the little tack room, rubbing saddle soap into the reins, bridles, harnesses, and fittings that filled the walls. The warm smell of leather and the tangy scent of polish filled the silence. It was even quieter there than in the main room of the stable. But there was no quiet in Phillip's mind.

He couldn't help wondering more about Bobby and the fire that killed his parents. Was Bobby home when it happened? Did he see it? Did he have brothers and sisters? What happened to them? Did he see his parents . . . after . . . ?

He couldn't help wondering, but he didn't want to ask. He was afraid of the answers he might get. Besides, Bobby wasn't talking. Phillip watched him while he rubbed a length of reins with polish. Bobby is a pretty good worker, he thought—when he isn't acting mean.

There was a sudden pounding at the door. "Bobby!" It was Pastor Olson's voice. "Bobby? Are you in there?"

A cloud of smoke puffed in through the doorway along with Pastor Olson. He grabbed Bobby and hugged him hard. "I've been looking everywhere for you!" he said. "Thank heavens you're safe. The steeple fell in through the church roof. We thought we got everybody out in time, but we couldn't find you."

"The steeple fell?" Phillip couldn't believe what the pastor was saying.

"Oh, Phillip, I thought you went with the family."

"Somebody had to stay with the horses," Phillip

explained. "But the church . . . ?" He'd always gone to Pastor Olson's church. If it was gone, what would he do?

"It looks like the north wall will go, too. And if there are more aftershocks, the rest may fall in. It is all a ruin." His voice trailed off. Then he shook his head and said, "Bobby, you must come home and eat. Then you can come with me or—"

The air shattered with the sound of a huge explosion. Dynamite? thought Phillip. A cannon?

"Steady, boys," Pastor Olson was saying. "They're blowing up buildings to try to stop the fires from spreading. The whole city is built of wood. There are gas fires starting up all over. There's no water. And this wind isn't helping either." He rubbed his face. "I don't know how they'll stop it."

"Is it coming this way?" Bobby's face was buried in Pastor Olson's jacket.

"Not now," he said. "Not yet, anyhow."

He looked at Phillip. "Is your house safe?" Phillip shook his head no. "Why don't you come and have lunch with Bobby?"

Phillip shook his head again. "I have to stay with the business," he said. He really didn't want to go out on the street and face the people, the noise, and the smell of smoke.

"Good point, son. Your father would be proud of you. People are already looting empty stores and homes, stealing anything they want. The police are shooting every looter they see."

"Oh, no!" Phillip hadn't thought of that danger. Pastor Olson looked sharply at him. "Can you protect yourself?" he asked.

Phillip knew what the minister was asking. He swallowed hard, thinking about the gun in the feed bag. "Yes," he said.

"Well, then. Are you hungry?"

Phillip's stomach growled. The pastor chuckled. "Bobby will be back with a sandwich for you."

"What about water?" Phillip called after them.

"There isn't any. All the water pipes in town were cracked open by the earthquake."

"But the horses will die without water!" Phillip cried. Pastor Olson stopped and thought for a minute.

"There's an old storage well behind our house. It hasn't been used in years. Maybe there's some water there. I'll have Bobby peek into it before he goes."

As he closed the door, Phillip wondered what he meant. Was Bobby going, too? It had been nice to have him here, Phillip thought. He blinked his eyes hard. Very nice.

Stampede!

Phillip went back to polishing the tack, but it wasn't the same. He was tired. He was hungry. And the smell of smoke kept getting stronger. When the last bridle was gleaming, he swept out both of the wagons.

Misty whinnied and rattled her water bucket. "Easy girl," Phillip said. "I'll get you some water soon." He tried turning the tap again. Nothing. Now all the horses were getting restless.

Where was Bobby? Phillip looked out the front window. He might have been waiting for hours. It might have been only half an hour. There was too much smoke in the sky to tell for sure.

Beauty was stamping the floor of her stall. "Whoa, there," Phillip called to her. Was it the smoke or the need for water that had her so spooked?

"Phillip!" Bobby finally yelled through the back door. "I've brought food!"

"The food can wait," Phillip said, opening the door. Bobby's smile disappeared, but Phillip didn't care. "Did you find any water in the old storage tank?" he asked.

"Well, yes . . ."

"Grab a couple of buckets and lead me there." And Phillip was out the door carrying three water buckets before Bobby could answer.

A noisy slurping sound was coming from every stall. The horses would need refills soon, Phillip thought, but for now, it was his turn. He finally stopped to eat. "Thanks," he said to Bobby. He bit into a cheese sandwich.

"What did the pastor mean about you going?" he asked.

"I'm heading out of town with Mr. Craig and his kids," he said. "Before supper. You want me to leave Buster with you?"

Phillip took a deep breath. It would be nice to have Buster for company—in case looters came. But it would be another animal to feed and water. "No, you take him," he finally answered. Alone again, he thought. "Is there more news from town?"

"Nothing good. The church is down. The school is on fire. And remember that big explosion we heard? It didn't work to stop the fire. It made it worse. Most of Chinatown is burning now."

"Chinatown!" Phillip thought about block after block of little wooden houses. No wonder there was so much smoke!

"I've got to go now," Bobby said. "Pastor told me to tell you to help yourself to the food in the kitchen and the water in the tank as long as it lasts." And then he was gone.

So was the church. And the school. All of Chinatown. His own house. The clock. The chandelier. Duchess. What would be left of his life when this was all over? he wondered. He felt like crying Phillip shook his head. At least the stable is safe, he told himself.

He looked at the new sign, gleaming in the smoky evening light. "You're all I have," he told it. "And you." He held out his hands and turned a great circle, looking at the horses in their stalls. "And I promise I won't let anything—anything—happen to any of you!"

Phillip filled the big watering trough from the parson's storage tank. It took almost an hour, hauling bucket after bucket across the street.

The road was still full of people fleeing from the fires. As twilight fell, the smoky glow from fires downtown painted the sky a strange dusky red. Phillip's shoulders ached from carrying water. His hands stung where the handles of the heavy buckets had bitten in. But he made another six trips, filling each horse's bucket to the top for the night.

He was sure he would fall asleep the moment he lay down in the soft hay on the tack room floor. It didn't work that way. When he closed his eyes, he thought about looters. He got up, checked the door, and brought his father's gun into the tack room with him.

When he tried to sleep again, he thought about Sundays without church. About Septembers without school. About a family without a home. And about his own family. Where were they? What would they find at Aunt Eleanor's? Was the earthquake there? Were fires burning everywhere around the world?

At last Phillip stood up and stretched. He brushed the hay off his overalls and wandered over to Linen's stall. The white horse reached her head over the door to nuzzle him. "No carrots, girl," he told her. "Just me." He leaned his cheek against her warm neck for a long, long time. The good smell of horse and Linen's strong, even pulse filled his mind.

Phillip awakened with a start. He'd dozed off just standing there! "Thanks, Linen," he murmured. "I think I can sleep now." He pulled a pile of horse blankets over and curled up on the floor with his back against Linen's stall.

Finally it was morning. The sky was smoky, but the wind had shifted. When would Papa get back? Phillip worried. He mucked the stalls—all except Duchess's. He fed and watered the horses, and still Papa hadn't come. He swept the floor, looking over his shoulder at the front door. No Papa. He fed himself over at the parson's kitchen.

Now what? Phillip wondered. He took out a can of varnish and a paintbrush. Then he pulled the new stable sign out to the backyard and propped it up in the sunlight. His eyes stung with the smoke, but the wind was blowing hard and hot again. Maybe the fire would blow away, he thought.

He dipped the brush into the paint can and pulled a smooth, glossy layer of varnish across the lettering. The gold words MACMILLAN AND SON glittered in the sunshine under the shiny new coat. "Beautiful," Phillip breathed as the lettering of LIVERY STABLE came alive. He laid brushful after brushful across the sign, overlapping each stroke just enough to cover. He knew there was no way to fix the varnish if it didn't go on just right.

The words BICYCLE REPAIR didn't look as good, he thought. But Papa had wanted them there.

He stood to inspect his work. "Oh, no!" he groaned. Flakes of ash were catching in the sticky varnish. He couldn't pick them out without leaving a smudge in the smooth coat. More ashes blew through the yard. The wind had changed, and it was blowing hard. Phillip looked up into the sky and saw billows of smoke overhead. "Great Scott!" he cursed. How close *was* the fire?

The horses were frightened, too. He could hear the restless drumming of their hooves and a chorus of whinnies.

Phillip ran in through the stable and on out the front door. The sky was thick with smoke and ashes were falling all around. A low roaring sound filled the air. People were running up the street now, not walking. "Where is it, Mrs. Taylor?" he called to the old lady. She was pulling the blind cocker along as fast as he could move.

"Heading this way," she called. "You better leave town!"

"How close is it?" he yelled at a soldier who was hurrying people along.

"Four blocks away," he told Phillip. "But she's burning faster than anything I've ever seen."

An explosion down the street rocked both of them. Linen neighed and Phillip ran back to calm the stableful. "Easy, now, easy," he said. Smoke was pouring in through the open door. The horses pricked their ears toward his voice—a voice they knew. But they still danced in their stalls in fear.

"Phillip!" Papa's voice called from the door.

"Papa!" Phillip ran to push open the carriage door. Papa drove the buggy inside. Before his father could set down the reins, Phillip had jumped onto the rig and was hugging him. "They say we have to go. We can't leave the stable!"

"We might have to," Papa said.

"No!" Phillip cried. "It's all we have left. The house is gone. The school. The church. We can't let the stable go. We can't!"

Another explosion split the air. Linen reared in her stall. Beauty's hooves crashed against her door as she tried to kick her way out. "Too close," said Papa.

"What is that?" A roaring filled Phillip's ears. It was a horrible sound. Was it from the explosion or was that the sound of the fire itself? Phillip couldn't tell.

"Who's in charge here?" A soldier stood in smoke in the doorway.

"I am," Papa said.

"You have to leave. Now. We're bombing the whole street to stop the fire."

"No!" screamed Phillip.

"How long do we have?" asked Papa.

"Half an hour. Maybe," the soldier said.

"We won't go!" Phillip yelled at him as he turned to leave.

"Then you'll die with your horses." The soldier's answer was swallowed by the strange roaring out on the street.

"But Papa . . ." Phillip started to plead. His father was already heading for the tack room.

"Help me load the bicycle tools into the buggy!" he called back to Phillip.

"What about the horses? And the tack? We can't be a stable without the horses!" But Papa had hauled out the boxes of bicycle parts and was heaving them into the buggy.

"We can't take everything, son. I can do bicycle repairs anywhere." He swung an armful of bicycle tires into the buggy. "And I bet I can work on those new automobiles, too. That's the future."

Phillip shook his head. Not that! Not automobiles! Papa was driving the buggy out the carriage door. Phillip stood in the middle of the stable. "You can't just let the horses die!" he screamed after him. He began throwing the stall doors open, one after another.

"Go, Linen!" he yelled, and smacked her smooth neck. Beauty broke out of her stall at a gallop, and Joe lunged out into the smoky room. Phillip slammed the stall doors behind them. The roaring of the fire and the horses' hooves filled the stable. "Get out!" Phillip yelled at Misty.

She backed farther into the safety of her stall. Phillip took off his cap and hit her with it. "Go!" he screamed. She reared. He held a grain bag over her eyes and pulled her past the door. "Go!" he yelled again.

And then they were gone. The stable was empty except for the terrible roaring. Phillip ran out onto the street, grabbing the horses' halters on the way. In the confusion, the horses had headed down toward the fire. Now Linen wheeled and came back up the road at Phillip. The rest followed. People screamed and jumped out of their way. "Stampede!" a soldier yelled, and aimed his gun at the big white horse.

Phillip didn't think. He stepped out in front of the horses, shouting "Easy, fellas." He stood still in the confusion of smoke and moving bodies. "Whoa, now. Easy." Phillip felt for calm. He *knew* calm. He tried to make Linen feel it, too.

And she did. The great horse slowed in front of him. Beauty stopped behind her. Then Joe settled in and the rest of the horses formed a tight herd. Phillip reached up and clipped a rope to Linen's halter.

"Thank you, girl," he whispered and pulled her away from the fire. "Let's just walk now."

Papa grabbed Beauty's halter, and passed Phillip a handful of lead ropes. "There might be time to tie them to the buggy," he said. "If you want to take them along."

In minutes, they were headed out of the city. Phillip

was sitting in the back of the buggy, facing the horses. "You sure do have a way with them," Papa said quietly.

I *do*, Phillip realized. I do have a way with horses. The knowing of it filled him with joy. Everything—everything—else is gone, he thought. But I still have this. And nothing can ever take it away.

A sharp explosion rocked the street behind them. "Easy now, fellas," Phillip said. "Easy."

ABOUT THIS BOOK

The earthquake struck at 5:12 A.M. on April 18, 1906. It lasted only a minute, but the fires it started raged for three days. The disaster killed 667 people. It destroyed the homes and businesses of 250,000 San Franciscans.

Why was it so bad? Back in 1906, people hadn't tried to make earthquake-proof buildings or water supplies. The Red Cross wasn't organized to help people in such huge disasters yet. The scientists had no idea why earthquakes happened. They did not know about continental drift or fault lines. They had not invented the Richter scale for measuring the strength of quakes. All these things happened after—and because of—the terrible losses of the San Francisco Earthquake.

Knowing when an earthquake is going to happen would save lives. To try to predict earthquakes, some scientists are studying how shock waves travel through the earth in front of quakes. Others are looking at the patterns of earthquakes or the movements of the continents themselves. Still other scientists are studying how animals know that an earthquake is about to happen.

For somehow animals do. Mice have been seen running in circles before earthquakes in China. Before the San Francisco Earthquake, dogs really did bark all night, and the horses wouldn't settle down. That much of my story is absolutely true.

So is the fire, the lack of water, the rush out of the city, and the bombing of Van Ness. I made up Phillip, his father, and pesty little Chester. To make the story as real as I could, I visited San Francisco and read the stories written by survivors of the great quake. I talked to fire fighters about how a huge fire really sounds. Stable owners and veterinarians told me how horses act when they are frightened or hurt. And I watched films of earthquakes, with people falling over and cans bouncing off store shelves.

The earthquake I wrote about was one of the strongest ones the United States has had—so far. Stresses are building up again in the great faults that cut through California. There have been many smaller quakes, but everybody wonders about the next "big one." When will it happen? We don't know, but we are as ready for it as we can be, thanks to the lessons learned in 1906.

K.V.K.